In loving memory of
Deirdre Redden —J. L.

For my children, Oshi and Oona,
I love you both with all my heart —H. C. B.

VIKING
An imprint of Penguin Random House LLC, New York

First published in the United States of America by Viking,
an imprint of Penguin Random House LLC, 2022

Text copyright © 2022 by Janet Lawler
Illustrations copyright © 2022 by Holly Clifton-Brown

Visit us online at penguinrandomhouse.com.

Library of Congress Cataloging-in-Publication Data is available.

Manufactured in Spain

ISBN 9780593326756

1 3 5 7 9 10 8 6 4 2

EST

Edited by Liza Kaplan
Design by Monique Sterling
Text set in Chaparral Pro

Artwork created using hand- and digital-painting techniques
with digital collaging in Adobe Photoshop.

OCEANS OF LOVE

Written by
JANET LAWLER

Illustrated by
HOLLY CLIFTON-BROWN

VIKING

Imagine moms beneath the waves
with lots of love to share.
Whatever might they say or do
to show how much they care?

Hermit crab shops here and there
to find a roomy shell.

She gently backs her baby in.
"Now, doesn't that fit well!"

Mother minnow darts and dips
in every tidal pool
to place her little swimmers in
the perfect minnow school.

Manta mama flaps her fins
to teach her tiny ray
graceful moves to swim and skim
and glide around all day.

Mother clam may tell her tots,
"Now, hurry, open wide!"

Dinner gets delivered when
there's plankton on the tide.

Dolphin playdates last all day,
and Mom keeps kiddies busy
doing twists, and jumps, and flips
till everyone is dizzy.

Octopus has many arms
to choose a hidden spot

where wee ones get untangled
if they're tied up in a knot.

Mother whale will blow her top
to spout her special love.

Her calf stays snuggled by her side
or, sometimes, just above.

Mama shark says, "Hold your fins
above the water line!"
She keeps her pups together
as they're heading out to dine.

Barnacle assures her young
it's quite all right to cling—

to rocks and docks and crates and gates,
in fact, most any thing.